Emma
and the Coyote
the

By Margriet Ruurs
Illustrations by Barbara Spurll

Stoddart
Kids
TORONTO • NEW YORK

To Charlene, Diane and all
the other librarians who bring
books and kids together.
— M.R.

To Alice and Victoria.
— B.S.

Text copyright © 1999 by Margriet Ruurs
Illustrations copyright © 1999 by Barbara Spurll

We acknowledge the Canada Council for the Arts and the
Ontario Arts Council for their support of our publishing program.

Published in Canada in 1999 by
Stoddart Kids,
a division of Stoddart Publishing Co. Limited
34 Lesmill Road
Toronto, ON M3B 2T6
Tel (416) 445-3333 Fax (416) 445-5967
E-mail Customer.Service@ccmailgw.genpub.com

Distributed in Canada by
General Distribution Services
325 Humber College Blvd.,
Toronto, ON M9W 7C3
Tel (416) 213-1919 Fax (416) 213-1917
E-mail Customer.Service@ccmailgw.genpub.com

Published in the United States in 1999 by
Stoddart Kids,
a division of Stoddart Publishing Co. Limited
180 Varick Street, 9th Floor
New York, New York 10014
Toll free 1-800-805-1083
E-mail gdsinc@genpub.com

Distributed in the United States by
General Distribution Services
85 River Rock Drive, Suite 202
Buffalo, New York 14207
Toll free 1-800-805-1083
E-mail gdsinc@genpub.com

Canadian Cataloguing in Publication Data
Ruurs, Margriet, 1952–
Emma and the coyote

ISBN 0-7737-3140-7

I. Spurll, Barbara.   II. Title.

PS8585.U97E45 1999   jC813'.54   C98-931790-0
PZ7.R88Em 1999

Printed and bound in Hong Kong by

Book Art Inc., Toronto

Emma fitted on her nest like the lid on a cookie jar. She was daydreaming with all the other chickens in the coop. Outside, the rooster kept watch over ten dandelion chicks.

Suddenly, Emma heard the farmer's voice. "You keep a close
eye on those chicks, fella," he said. "There has been a coyote
close by . . . too close for comfort."

Emma went outside, blinking in the bright sunlight.

She watched the farmer fix a hole in the fence. He pulled the wires tight and nailed them to a post.

"Tok!" said Emma. "That won't keep us safe from the coyote." When the farmer left, Emma stuffed sticks of straw into the holes in the wire.

The next day, Emma was scuttling in the garden. She ran around radishes. She munched on marigolds, and picked bugs off beets. She was just about to snap at a grasshopper, when the rooster yelled, "Cockadooooh! Cockadooooh-doooh-doooh!" Then he sprinted for the chicken coop.

Emma looked up and saw a bushy tail on the other side of the garden. All the other chickens scurried away as fast as they could.

But not Emma.

Emma ran to the house and hopped onto the apple crate under the kitchen window. She jumped up and down, down and up, up and down.

"Why it's Emma!" the farmer's wife cried. "She's bouncing like a ball!"

The farmer's wife ran outside and spotted the coyote sneaking closer. She picked up a stone and hurled it. The coyote ran away.

"Good girl, Emma!" said the farmer's wife. "But you watch out! Coyotes are smarter than chickens."

"Tok!" said Emma. She walked back to the chicken coop with her beak in the air.

The following afternoon, Emma and the other chickens were looking for good things to eat in the pig pen. Emma wrestled with worms and picked at potato peels. She was just gobbling up some corn when she heard a loud commotion.

The pigs snorted. The rooster crowed. The chickens clucked after him as he darted inside the coop.

But not Emma.

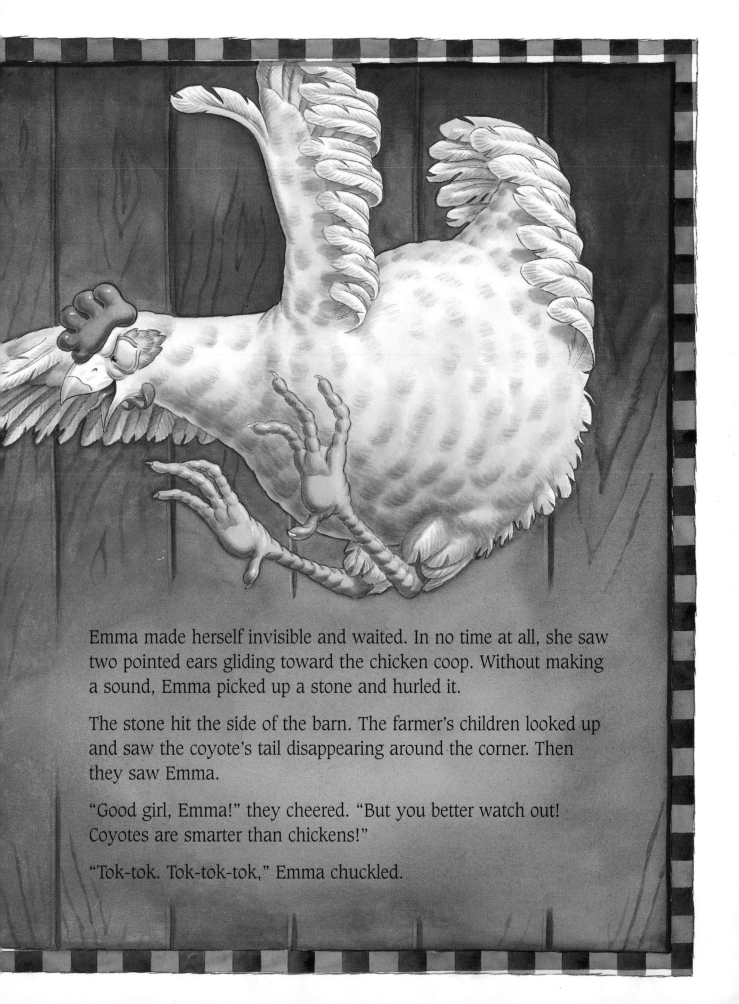

Emma made herself invisible and waited. In no time at all, she saw two pointed ears gliding toward the chicken coop. Without making a sound, Emma picked up a stone and hurled it.

The stone hit the side of the barn. The farmer's children looked up and saw the coyote's tail disappearing around the corner. Then they saw Emma.

"Good girl, Emma!" they cheered. "But you better watch out! Coyotes are smarter than chickens!"

"Tok-tok. Tok-tok-tok," Emma chuckled.

The next morning, the coyote was back. This time, Emma spied him in the orchard where the other chickens were eating bugs under the cherry trees. Emma raced over, wings flapping. "Tok, TOK-TOK, **TOK!**" she shouted. She made such a racket that the rooster and the chickens dashed away.

But not Emma.

Emma hid behind a tree trunk and stood still. Then she hurried to another tree. She zigged left and zagged right, from one tree to another, until the coyote wasn't sure where she was anymore. He twitched his nose and sniffed the air. He came closer, then closer, right to the tree where Emma was hiding. He licked his lips.

Just when Emma had nowhere to run, she heard the farmer's children ask, "Is that a chicken by the cherry tree?"

"It's Emma!" gasped the farmer's wife. She flung a stick at the coyote, who ran away.

"Emma, Emma!" the farmer's wife panted. "You better watch out! Coyotes are definitely smarter than chickens!"

At that very moment, Emma had nothing to say — not even one tiny, little tok.

The farmer knew the coyote would get the chickens sooner or later, so he brought home a trap. If he could catch the coyote, he would take him far away from the farm and set him free in the woods. The farmer placed the trap under the magnolia tree.

No sooner was the trap set than Emma went to check it out. The other chickens were afraid to go near it.

But not Emma.

Emma fluttered into the
lower limbs of the magnolia
tree. She sat there waiting
on a swaying branch.

The sun was warm and Emma began to daydream. She pretended to be a giant magnolia blossom. She didn't notice the coyote creep into the yard. The coyote didn't see the giant magnolia either. He smelled the grass and sniffed the tree trunk. Emma teetered back and forth, trying to hold onto her branch.

Then the coyote spotted the trap. It smelled good. There was food inside it, but he was suspicious. He would not step inside. Coyotes are too smart for that.

Suddenly, the wind picked up and Emma's branch swayed even more. She lost her balance, and a huge, feathery, flapping, clucking, magnolia blossom tumbled out of the tree. It landed on the coyote and pecked him hard on the backside! The coyote yelped and jumped forward — straight into the trap.

Slam!

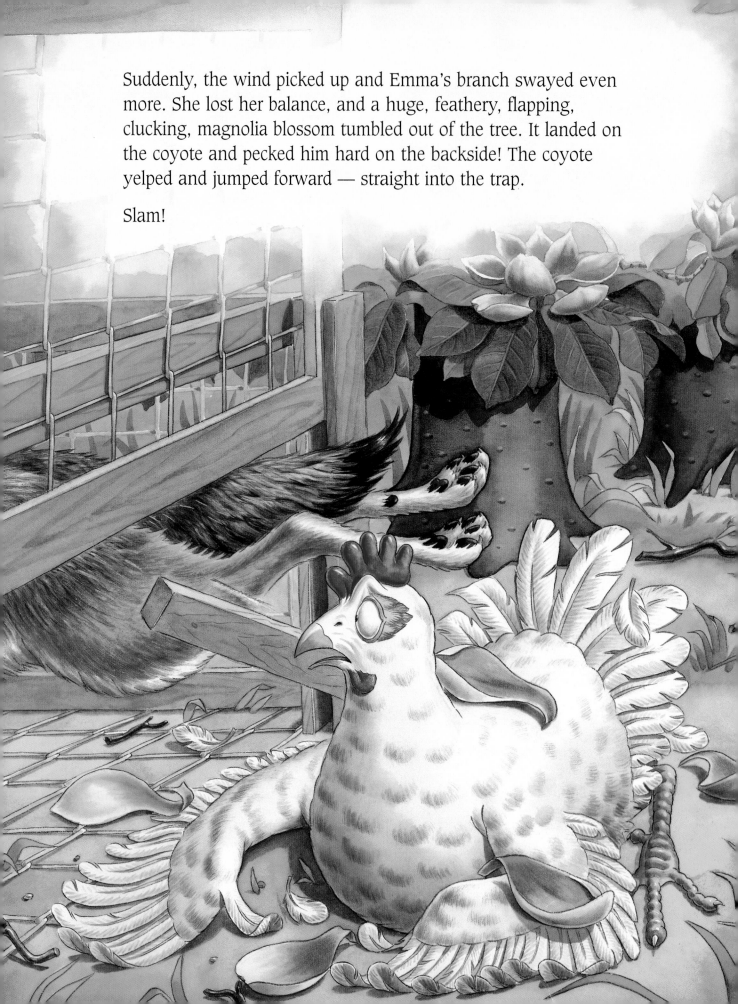

Everyone heard the noise and came running.
"All right, Emma!" they cried.

Other chickens would have been flustered. But not Emma. Emma
fluffed herself up and looked down her beak at the coyote. Then,
on legs that trembled just a little, she marched past the rooster, the
chickens, the ten dandelion chicks, and went inside the chicken
coop.

Emma settled on her nest for a well-earned rest. Soon dreams of bugs, beetles and feathery magnolia blossoms floated in her head. "Tok-tok. Tok-tok . . . tok . . .," she chuckled as she heard the farmer, the farmer's wife and the farmer's children talking outside.

"Well, what do you know," they had to admit. "Some chickens *are* smarter than coyotes!"